MISS EMILY

MISS EMILY

Burleigh Mutén

ILLUSTRATED BY Matt Phelan

CANDLEWICK PRESS

Text copyright © 2014 by Burleigh Mutén
Illustrations copyright © 2014 by Matt Phelan

The note from Emily Dickinson on page 82 is reprinted by permission of the publishers from *The Letters of Emily Dickinson*, edited by Thomas H. Johnson, Cambridge, MA: Belknap Press/Harvard University Press, copyright © 1958, 1986 by the President and Fellows of Harvard College; 1914, 1924, 1932, 1942 by Martha Dickinson Bianchi; 1952 by Alfred Leete Hampson; 1960 by Mary L. Hampson.

The poem excerpt beginning "We never know how high we are" (J 1176/F 1197) on page 124 is reprinted by permission of the publishers and the trustees of Amherst College from *The Poems of Emily Dickinson*, edited by Thomas H. Johnson, Cambridge, MA: Belknap Press/Harvard University Press, copyright 1951, © 1955, 1979, 1983 by the President and Fellows of Harvard College.

First edition 2014

Library of Congress Catalog Card Number 2013943089
ISBN 978-0-7636-5734-5

13 14 15 16 17 18 MVP 10 9 8 7 6 5 4 3 2 1

Printed in York, PA, U.S.A.

This book was typeset in Hightower.

Candlewick Press
99 Dover Street
Somerville, Massachusetts 02144

visit us at www.candlewick.com

For my boys,
and in memory of MacGregor Jenkins
B. M.

CONTENTS

Introduction

This tale of small-town high adventure is told by young MacGregor Jenkins, the pastor's son who lived across the street from the Dickinsons of Amherst more than one hundred years ago.

Mac and his sister, Sally, regularly postured themselves as pirates, cowboys, gypsies, bandits, and heroes along with their neighbors Ned and Mattie Dickinson. In the woods and shrubs surrounding their homes, these four friends superimposed fantasy over reality along with Ned and Mattie's aunt Emily Dickinson, who lived next door. Long after Miss Emily had withdrawn from Amherst society to live a private life, she continued to enjoy the imagination and playful company of her young neighbors.

Although the characters and circumstance of this story are based in reality, I too have accepted childhood's invitation to lay a veil over reality for a bit of dedicated play. Characters take on stage names as the tale unfolds.

DRAMATIS PERSONAE

MISS EMILY
   Queen Prosperina

MacGREGOR JENKINS
   King Boaz the Brave

NED DICKINSON
   Señor Ranchero; the ringmaster

MATTIE DICKINSON
   Miss Swiftly

SALLY JENKINS
   Sal the Gal

1 · The Invitation

Ned knocked on the door.
"Saddle up, Mac!
We're invited
to the Mansion!"

I stepped outside
and swiftly
swung my hand
up to my forehead,
shooting it skyward
in a quick salute.

"Charge!" called Ned
over his shoulder,
turning his horse
toward the street.

I grabbed the reins
of my imaginary mare
and leaned into the wind.

We kicked into a gallop,
and circled round to the back
of Ned's house.
We dismounted
at the woodpile —
a mountain of logs
where all good plans are made.

"Here's the invitation," said Ned,
pulling a small white scrap
of paper from his pocket.

Dear Boys, he read,
Please — do join me in the garden
with the quiet pace
of the unseen unsung
slippery slugs who slide
through the grass after the rain.
Ever your devoted, Miss E.

"*Hooray!*" shouted Mattie
as she leaped from the shed's low roof
and landed with a thud in front of Ned.

"We shall approach the Mansion at once!"
  she declared, hands on her hips.
"Hurry on to the far side
  of the fence behind the barn!
  We'll cross over to the garden,
  tree to tree,
  one at a time,
  to the Great Pink Bush."

  Ned stepped toward Mattie,
  backing her up
  to the wall of the shed.

"Her note says, 'Dear *Boys*,'" said Ned,
  his blue eyes flashing
  from Mattie to me
  and once again to Mattie.
"*Girls* are *not* invited."

  Mattie cinched the drawstring
  of her hat strap and strode
  toward Ned so fast
  he backed right up
  to the woodpile.

"She calls us *all* boys, Ned.
  You know that.

Let's be on with it!

Come on out, Sally!"
ordered Mattie to the woodpile.
And out strode Sally, my own sister,
from her hiding place behind the wood,
where she'd been waiting for her cue.

"Sisters," said Sally
  in her most Mother-like voice,
"are always invited to the Mansion.
  You *boys* know that.
  Two sisters *live* in the Mansion —
  Miss Emily *and* Miss Vinnie.
  Let's be on with it!
  She's surely waiting
  for us this very moment."

I stepped forward, harrumphing like Father,
and climbed the wobbling woodpile
till I stood above those three,
taller now than Ned.

"Miss Emily did make a request this time,
  didn't she?" I dared them. "She asked us to be slugs!"

And so four silent slugs slid behind the fence
behind the barn, out into the open —
stretching, trying not to use arms or hands,

as we slithered across the cool, dewy grass
to the Great Pink Bush.

I glanced up as I wiggled,
feeling my shirt dampen —
and there she was —
kneeling as always when she gardened,
protecting her crisp white dress
with a rough blue apron.
She was trying not to giggle,
but her shaking shoulders
showed the truth.

Miss Emily put down her trowel,
brushed her hair from her face, and stood.
She paused and squinted at the hills,
looking upward at the clouds for a moment
before her eyes met ours,
and she began to applaud.

"Bravo! to the slug theatre." She laughed,
  her brown eyes crinkling as she smiled.
"Bravo! to the wriggling, giggling slugs."

She was trying not to giggle.

2 · The Plan

We laughed as we ran to her blanket.
Mattie and Sally claimed their places at her side;
Ned and I flourished our hats
and bowed at the blanket's edge.

"Please sit down," Miss Emily urged.
"I have News and a Plan," she said,
 tilting her head toward the house,
 nodding her slowest of nods,
 so we knew without words
 that it was a Secret Plan.

"Now, My-Mice-on-Christmas-Morning,
 you four dearest happy friends,
 it is my great joy to inform you

of the vast surprise that rushes
roaring toward us this very moment!

"Two hundred legs and fifty heads,
some sleek, some curly,
some most certainly red!
The smallest —
smaller than our youngest,
our brave Mac.
The tallest — mighty enough
to give each of us the sillies, and if
we are not careful, a snort and a whack!"

Miss Emily watched us,
her smile widening for a second or two,
waiting for us to guess her riddle —
but before we could speak,
she burst out with
"I cannot bear it!"

Her whole body shivered as she said,
"It's the *circus*!
The circus is coming on the rails tonight.
I've just heard."

"Yes, yes, Aunt Emily,
   that is the news," said Mattie.
"*What* is the plan?"

"The Plan is this:
   the circus cars will arrive at midnight.
   I've seen them from my window every spring.
   The town is as still as an unplanted seed.
   The street itself is asleep,
   and I — the solitary witness.

"*This* year . . ." She paused, smoothing her skirt.
"Oh, look, the bees have found the yellow tulips."

"Aunt Emily, please!" said Ned.
"This year, what? This year *what* is the plan?"

"*Ah,* yes, this year, I propose you gypsies join me!
   After the second whistle and the hiss of the steam,
   we five wily ones will watch
   horses and monkeys,
   and if Fortune smiles —
   an elephant shall strut from the cars!
   We'll see the gypsies of our clan,
   the ones who travel far and farther
   than we Amherst gypsies can."

Ned bounced to his feet.
"It's a great, gleaming plan!" he cried.
"Gypsies tonight!
All ready for the midnight train,
put your hands atop mine," he ordered.

"Gypsies tonight!" we all cried.

3 · Waiting for the Grandfather

"What will Father say?" I asked Sally
  as we crossed the dusty street to home.

"We cannot tell him, Mac. Nor Mother.
  Their worries would prevent the plan.
  We shall be night watchmen
  in our beds tonight, waiting
  for the grandfather in the hall
  to tell us when it's time."

"What if I fall asleep and don't wake up?" I asked.

"I will wake you with a nudge, Mac.
  Just think of it!
  We will be the first in town to see the circus!"

"But what if someone sees us out alone at night?"

"Then whoever might be seeing us
will also see Miss Emily.
No one shall wonder if
we are with a grown-up."

"Of course." I nodded.
"We shall have Miss Emily."

I lay in bed, listening.
I heard six horses pass the house
and two carriages.
I named the constellations and their stars,
the countries of Europe and their cities.
I named the states and their capitals,
and just as I started with the kings
and queens of England,
Grandfather Clock began
his slow, soft call of eleven o'clock.
I counted with him,
my excitement growing,
knowing that at the last gong,
Sally would cross the hall,
making her way to me.
But when she didn't come,
I slipped into my clothing
and went to her.

Sally's eyes flew open
when I touched her arm.
"Mac," she groaned,
"my belly hurts.
 I can't go with you.
 You'll have to be brave
 and meet Miss Emily
 and the others by yourself."

"I couldn't!" I protested.
"You have to come!"

"Look, Mac!" she whispered, sitting up
 as she grabbed something from her bed.
"It's Mother's old purple shawl.
 Perfect for your cloak."
 I was astounded and enticed —
 Sally never let any of us use the purple shawl.
 She quickly laid it on my shoulders,
 clasped it at my chest with a shiny brooch,
 and tied a deep-green scarf around my head.
 The soft velvet of the cloak draped below my knees,
 its silver fringe sweeping my hands and lower legs,
 and I was a gypsy king! I had to go!

"You are thoroughly grand," said Sally
 in a hushed voice. "It is nearly the hour

"You are thoroughly grand," said Sally.

for our distant family to arrive.
You must be gracious and
welcome them properly
to our little country town.
Do not forget your cane, sir!"

I took the back stairs to the kitchen,
slid through the pantry to the hall,
and slipped out the side door.
From the dark veranda, the backyard shadows
reached out like sharks and whales in the blackest sea.
I leaped from the top step like a pirate jumping ship,
and swam across the bay to the island —
up a hill to the fence that beckoned beside the barn
and through the door that Miss Emily
had promised would be open.

4 · The Naming

There she sat on her father's workbench,
a lantern at her side, hands folded in her lap.

"Miss Emily," I said, bowing before her,
catching a glimpse of her pink-slippered feet.

"Your journey was a safe one, I presume?" she asked.
"But where, sir, is your sister?
And the others? Where could those rascals be?"

As if called by her words,
Ned and Mattie clambered through the door,
Ned in his wide-brimmed hat and
Mattie wrapped in a feathered shawl.

There she sat on her father's workbench.

"Dear me, Miss Mattie." Miss Emily laughed.
"How ever did you manage running
  without taking flight?"

"I held her hand, Aunt Emily," said Ned.
"I held her down to earth! Look, Mac!
  I've made the old calfskin from the stable into a cloak."

"That mangy old thing
  is what took us so long,"
moaned Mattie.
"Ned said he wasn't coming
  if he couldn't make it into his cloak.
  Where's Sally?"

"Yes, where is dear Sally?" asked Miss Emily.
"She must be ill to miss this mischievous treat!"

I deepened my voice to sound like Doc Gridley
and said, "Too ill to travel now.
Bedridden and woozy with waves of willies."

"Hmm," said Miss Emily,
  tying a long silk scarf around her head
  so it covered all of her chestnut hair.
"It's a turban!" she announced.
"From the Orient!"

I didn't like her turban.
With her hair all gone and her cheeks so wide,
Miss Emily looked like a different person —
until she giggled her tinkling laugh,
and there she was again,
leaping down from the workbench onto the floor,
pulling the folds of her cape close to herself
as she looked each of us in the eye.

"Call me Prosperina — Queen of the Night, if you please,
  for I will charm the diamond vipers
  till they dance tonight!"
And she wiggled her arm and her hand like a snake.

She strode before us,
slowly looking each of us up and down,
motioning for us to turn around
so she could see the entirety of our costumes.

"You, sir," she said, nodding at Ned,
"are clearly Señor Ranchero — the fastest rider
  in the American West, who will dazzle us all
  with your daring equestrian team!

"And you," she said, turning to Mattie,
"you are Miss Swiftly,

the world-renowned half-bird, half-girl
from the Amazon Jungle!"

At last when she stopped at my eyes,
Queen Prosperina announced,
"None other than my king —
Boaz the Brave,
revered among gypsies the world over
for your courage and kindness
in the face of Incomparable Danger!"

We bowed to each other,
and the Queen blew out the light.
I reached for her hand
as she waved our scout Ranchero
to lead us into the night.

5 · The Open Moonlight

It was cool, not cold.
Nor was there a breeze.

Prosperina put her hand up to her ear
and whispered,
"The tree frogs' chorus!
A full applause!
Those dear small things
all a-jingle for our boldness
and our royal finery!
Oh, dear me!
I forgot our beast!" she cried,
dropping my hand.
She dashed back to the barn
and returned in a flash
with Carlo
lumbering behind.

"He knows these fields night and day
  better than we," said Prosperina.
"He'll let us know if trouble's near."

Ranchero shook Carlo's floppy ears
  as he muttered, "Good dog, Carlo.
Good old boy."

"Take the hill path," commanded Prosperina.
"We won't want to wake
  every poor creature in the pound.
  Oh, that we could free the lot of them!" she murmured,
looking sadly at the fenced-in yard
  of the town's dog pound.

Carlo grumbled at Ranchero's side,
  and up we went on the hedge-lined path
  that edged the garden.

I ran to keep up with Prosperina.
She pulled me on beside her,
  so fast I worried I might fall.

Through the woods we were swift,
  up to the crest of the hill.
  It was so dark, I was glad to see
  the silhouetted rim

Through the woods we were swift.

of the Pelham Hills
in the rising moonlight.

Then across the meadow
and back into the brushy forest,
we four ran in silence,
the soft spring earth
a carpet for our feet.

We stopped at the tree line,
safe in the shadows.
"We must consider the open moonlight,"
warned Prosperina.
"And we must contrive."

My breath reached into the cool air
in tiny puffs, and then I saw
that we had traveled far already,
for there — just down the hill,
across the quiet road,
its roof gleaming silver —
was the train station.

A small flickering light within
reminded me that Draper,
the stationmaster,
was waiting, too.

Queen Prosperina giggled.
"Dear old Draper
  will come running
  out of the station
  when he hears the whistle cry!

"You'll see him twitter and jitter
  as he tries with all his might
  to stand stately in his uniform
  as the great elephant and the tiger
  and the rest disembark."

The rest! I wondered.
What else would there be?

6 · Severity and Consequence

"We will see it all,"
  the Queen went on,
  nodding slowly to herself,
"the horde of horses
  and their riders,
  the fortune-teller
  and the strongest man alive.
  We shall see it all,
  yes, we shall,
  and for all that we shall see,
  We Shall Not Be Seen,
  my daring friends,
  my king and my fast scout,
  and you, my beautiful bird-girl."

"What are you saying, Aunt?"
  demanded Mattie.
"I'm not hiding
  when they arrive!
  How ever could we greet the gypsy clan?
  I will not be rude. I *will* greet them."

"Surely you, Miss Swiftly,"
  said Miss Emily,
  stroking Mattie's feathers,
"know the Severity
  and Consequence
  of Mr. Draper spying us —
  out and about at night.
  Why, dear ones,
  our dear Draper
  would most certainly
  without hesitation,
  even if he is filled with regret,
  find it His Sober Civic Duty
  to tell the Entire Town
  of our Great Adventure
  should he happen
  upon our gypsy band.

"Why, I fear we would —
  all four — Be Obliged

to wear mud on Sunday —
if we are allowed at all
out of our rooms that day!"

I shivered,
thinking of my father's face
on Sunday morning —
the whole town knowing
the pastor's son
had slipped out at night
with a band of gypsies
while his father slept.

"Onward now!"
commanded Prosperina.
"To Big Beech!"
I startled as she jerked me onward,
galloping across the meadow
toward the grove of chestnuts
and Big Beech, the oldest giant
this side of town,
whose lowest branches
reached for the ground,
creating a perfect cave around us.

"What good fortune!" cried Prosperina.
"Just look," she said,

lifting her chin toward the station
across the silent road.

"Quite excellent, Ranchero!" she said,
    turning toward Ned.
"Clearly your cavalry years
    have honed your talents as a scout!
    We shall await the train right here."

7 · Big Beech

I swung my leg over a branch,
straddled it like a saddle
and snuggled my back against
Big Beech's smooth broad trunk.
I closed my eyes and heard
twigs snap and leaves crackle
as the others moved about.

I opened my eyes
searching for Miss Emily.
Ranchero was stretched flat
on the earth looking like a log,
Carlo — a hibernating bear at his side.
Miss Swiftly was perched
on the branch above me,

and Prosperina . . .
where had she gone?
I leaned forward
and turned from side to side
to find her standing on one foot
her arms poking out at the elbows.

"Practicing the flamingo," she said.

And even though I heard her voice
she still did not look like Miss Emily.
That thieving Oriental turban
had stolen her hair.
Her cloak rounded out her sides
so she looked too large.
I jumped down
and nearly knocked her over, pleading,
"A story, Miss Emily, please!
Tell us a story while we wait!"

"Why, King Boaz," she replied,
"you are correct to ask the jester
for diversion, but!
by the light of the moon —
will there be time for a story?
Please, sire, check your timepiece.

"Practicing the flamingo," she said.

I — forgetful as the wind —
have forgotten my own."

"Twelve to twelve," I announced,
conjuring a time, for I had no idea
what hour it really was.

"Why, yes, there shall be time
for one short tale.
Sit near me now."

8 · A Large Dream

"Once," she began,
  her voice low and slow.
"Not so long ago
  and not so far away,
  there was a horse
  named Edward."

Miss Emily paused,
taking hold of Carlo's
great wide head
with both her hands.
She brought her eyes
close to his,
gave him a short shake,
and continued.

"From the moment of his birth,
 Fortune smiled on Edward,
 for he was born inside a circus tent!
 Without question!
 destined for a life of greatness.

"This stallion Edward
 was trained to carry
 humans on his back.
 Not seated in a saddle
 don't you know!
 but Standing Humans,
 one
 atop
 the
 other,
 so Edward trotted
 round the ring, bearing
 a tower of three men —
 what a sight!
 The crowd was
 quite in love
 with Edward.
 How they crowed!"

"Aunt Emily,
 is there a bit of truth

to this story?"
demanded Mattie.

"Why, yes,
there may be
a bit of truth.
Listen, now.

"Edward was proud,
and his trainer,
Mr. John Bill Wrinkles,
was most deeply pleased.
Edward, however, after some time
was starstruck with a dream.

"'I should like to fly,'
he told John Bill.
'I see birds aloft and hear them sing.
I see men like you without a wing
hold the trapeze and whip across the tent.
I should like to feel the wind below me.
You have taught me all I know, John Bill.
Can you teach me this?'

"John Bill loved a challenge.
He smiled and said,

'Of course, Edward.
Of course, I will.'"

Ned sat up.
Carlo groaned and stretched,
and the train whistle split the night
with a long, shrill cry that sang to us,
and we were standing,
full of glee, forgetting there
had ever been a story about Edward.

"She's coming! The train is coming!"
Mattie squealed so loudly, Miss Emily
placed her palms
on Mattie's chest and back.

Mattie giggled right on
till Ned put his face directly in front of hers,
imitating their father's stern slow voice:
"Mar-tha Dick-in-son!
You *are* a lady!"

Mattie closed her mouth
and clapped her arms
to her sides.
Her eyes rolled
toward Miss Emily,

whose own eyes rolled
right on toward me.

"Hist whist! We must be off!"
 commanded Prosperina.
"Carlo, stay!" she ordered.
"We're all best blessed
 if you wait here.
 We shall return!"

9 · The Train

"Follow quickly!" she commanded,
  catching each one of us with her eyes.
Then she turned and swept down
the sloping meadow,
across the dusty road
to the back of the station,
where we flattened ourselves
against its wooden wall,
all in a row holding hands —
Miss Emily next to me,
then Mattie and Ned
in the dark safety of the station's shadow.

The whistle shrieked louder this time —
E-E-E-E-E-E-E-E —

and now I could see the train
*chunk-chunk-chink*ing toward us,
and the ground was shaking
and a roaring rushed into my ears
as the big black engine turned the curve.
It screeched and hissed its arrival,
so close I felt its heat brush my face.
The station wall behind us creaked
and trembled as the train slowed to a stop,
groaning like Carlo collapsing after a run.

Draper called to the engineer,
but none of us could see him,
for the first cars had passed the station.
Prosperina tugged my hand, inching toward
the corner of the wall so she could see.
Drawing herself back quickly, she whispered,
"We'll wait here as the animals are released
so we'll glimpse them all up close."

The burning coal fumes bit my nostrils,
and I could feel Mattie's feet a-tapping.
Men's voices began calling to one another,
and wooden doors slid apart, rattling and slamming
against the train cars. Horses whinnied.
I heard a big cat's grumbling growl.
And we waited.

When the circus folk and animals appeared,
our sleepy station became a boulevard
of people bustling, crowding one another
fast and slow, to and fro, laughing and talking,
and no one noticing the four of us.
There were more horses than I could count,
and an elephant as tall as the station, even taller,
swayed past us, turning in our direction,
its rubbery trunk reaching into the night.

Two tall men with bulging bellies laughed
so loudly as they approached the station
and us in its shadows, I was scared.
One of them stumbled, so the two banged heads
and one's cigar went flying,
its orange-red glowing tip
twirling through the air,
landing near Miss Emily's feet.
Her hand around mine jiggled
to the fast-paced tune she hummed
till the man lumbered on, unaware
of us or his lost cigar.

A tall wagon with bars
was slowly rolled down an incline
onto the platform by a group of men
hollering commands to one another.

"It's the tiger!"
  said the Queen, squeezing my hand.
"The tiger," I repeated to myself.

  We watched the rhinoceros roll by,
  and the hippopotamus,
  stunned by each one's oddly placed horns
  and bulging sides.

"What's here?" said someone with a laugh
  that made the Queen jump,
  her hand grabbing on to mine so tight,
  I almost pulled away until I saw this someone
  striding from the circus city street toward us.

"A family of local performers, eh? Look, Mama!
  It's the Amherst gypsies come to greet us!"

10 · Miz Rozalia

A big woman, round as pie,
swaggered over to us, smiling.
"Oh my, oh my, oh, so it is!
A whole family of 'em.
Kindly of you, very kindly.
Come out of them shadows
so we can see yuh!"

My feet were as heavy as rocks.
I was too scared to move, but
when the Queen and Mattie tugged—
away from the wall I floated like in a dream.
Ned put his arm around my shoulder, saying,
"It's all right, Mac. No one here will harm us."

The mama was talking
with Prosperina and Miss Swiftly.

"Look here," cried the someone,
  who was her son, I believe,
"what acts can yuh do?
  Maybe we can use yuh in the show."

"Oh, sir," said Prosperina,
"we are greeters, nothing more."

From what seemed nowhere,
  there in his uniform and cap
was Draper!
My feet, my legs,
  my arms and head
were all rock now.

Miss Emily stood tall
like a trickster trained for years
and bowed low before him.
When she rose, she stared at Draper
like a stranger straight on,
and said politely,
"Queen Prosperina, sir.
  I hope yuh'll be a-comin' to the show."

She swiveled on her heel
  like usual when she disappeared —
so fast, time sped up, leaving folks

wondering if they'd seen a woman
or a wisp of smoke.
She slid her arm beneath the mama's arm,
and we strode behind them
into the hubbub of people shouting,
Prosperina and the mama talking
like they'd been looking forward
to this meeting forever.
I began to wonder if we were going
to get into one of those wagons
and head for the fairgrounds
when the mama turned around
and stopped in front of me,
kneeling down to face me
as she took my hand,
turned it palm up,
and stroked it slowly,
leaning close to look.

"So, you're Boaz —
  King of the Brave." She laughed.
"I myself am known as Miz Rozalia."

"She's looking for your future,"
  whispered Mattie.

"She's a fortune-teller," said Ned.

11 · The Future Now

"Yes, sir, I see you're a brave one, Boaz.
and your hand's a-speakin'
that you're a storyteller, too.
Writin' books when you're a grown-up,
and a good long life is yours to boot!"

She smiled and her eyes crinkled like Miss Emily's,
and I wondered how she knew about my stories
and how I wanted to be a writer
when I had never told a soul.
I felt like she was my mama in that moment,
so when she opened her arms to hug me,
I just did the same!

"Excuse me, folks, you'd best be moving on now,"
directed Draper, leaning down to get a closer look at me.

"You're a storyteller, too."

"Come on, young-uns," said Miz Rozalia,
  standing a good head taller than Draper,
  placing an unfriendly stare in his direction.
"There's a heap o' work needin' us afore we sleep."

  She turned us away from Draper's gaze
  and pulled us into the crowd.

"Now, Miz Prosperina," said Miz Rozalia,
"you'd best be getting these youngsters off to bed
  afore someone local grabs a closer look at 'em."

  Miss Emily smiled.
"I'm Most Pleased to have made
  your Esteemed Acquaintance,"
  she said, nodding her respect,
"as are we all."

"Most grateful to know you," said Ned,
  bowing at the waist.

"Glory me," said Miz Rozalia,
  glancing down to her shoes.
"I expect I'll see y'all tomorrow
  at the Great Golden Menagerie and Circus,
  and when I do, I'll send yuh a wink
  so as no one knows we met tonight!"

She chuckled and turned,
swallowed by the bustling crowd.
Miss Emily squeezed my shoulders.

"Dear Mac! You are a writer!
I should have known!
Now . . ." she said, looking at the moon.

"Now what?" demanded Mattie.

Miss Emily looked shocked awake
from a dream too real to leave.

"To Carlo in the Cave!"

12 · The Tiger's Roar

We were running again,
Miss Emily pulling my hand.
She was a trout flitting from danger,
bolting across the soft dusty road,
rushing up the sloping meadow.

My breath was short.
My side pinched
and squeezed my ribs.
I had to slow down.

"Faster, my king!"
 she commanded,
"so we are not seen."
 I knew she meant Draper,

who stared so close,
I was sure he knew me.

I pressed my palm against
the knife-sharp ache
biting my side,
my breath ripping
through my throat.

How she ran! squeezing my hand,
urging, "Faster, Boaz! Faster!"

I pressed my palm hard
against my ribs
and ran faster
when I felt something round
and slippery beneath my foot
throwing me forward,
cutting my hand free
from Miss Emily's
so I hit the ground,
crying out
with no thought
of who might hear.

"It's Mac!" cried Miss Emily.
"He's fallen."

"Faster, my king!"

Carlo bellowed,
crashing through the meadow,
barking all the way.

"Carlo — hush *now*!
Be Still or you'll wake the town!"
Miss Emily hissed.

Carlo growled a sharp note at the night
and flopped down, licking my hand.

"Oh, my dear Mac,
dear, dear, and oh dear —
let's see you stand up."

I tried, but I could not.
Tears streamed down my cheeks.

"I'll carry him, Aunt," said Ned,
sliding his arm beneath my knees.
"Put your arm around my neck, Mac,
and we'll go directly to Big Beech.
You'll be fine — don't worry."

My ankle was on fire.
I didn't want to cry,
but the pain was a tiger's roar.

13 · News—Good and Bad

Ned stooped as we entered Big Beech,
holding me close to his chest
as he lowered me to the ground.

"Oh, my word,"
  Miss Emily murmured.
"Slip, slash, and balderdash!"
  She held my ankle in her cool hands,
  tilting it ever so slightly this way,
  now that way,
  now up and down.
  I pulled my breath in tight
  so as not to yelp.
  Miss Emily looked
  straight into my eyes.

"Slip, slash, and balderdash!"

She smiled her slimmest smile
and said,

"The Good News is this!
Your ankle is not broken.
Oh, I know it is howling,
but it is Not Broken.
It *will* Heal.

"The Bad News is thus!
Ned will carry you home
to the parsonage now.
I shall ring the bell
and make a clear confession to your father,
for I am the scheming source of this night's"—
she coughed—"deception.
It is I
who have
Most Selfishly
put You,
My Dearest Friends,
in harm's way.

"Now, Mattie dear,
run ahead directly
with Great Focused Care
to the icehouse

and then to Reverend Jenkins's
so we can stop Mac's ankle swelling
the moment the pastor sees us."

"I'm sorry, Miss Emily," I snuffled.
"I've ruined the Plan. And now
   Father will be furious
   and Ned's father, too.
   The whole town will know
   how horrible we are."

"Yes," said Miss Emily. "I suppose they will."

14 · Confession

Miss Emily banged on the kitchen door
and pulled it open,
not waiting for a reply
as she called out
in the loudest voice
I've ever heard her use.

"Reverend Jenkins! Mrs. Jenkins!
Come down at once!
It's Miss Emily!
Reverend! Mrs. Jenkins!
Please do hurry,
there's been . . .
an accident."

Miss Emily lit a lamp.
Its yellow light

threw shadows
on her face,
her mouth a straight line,
her eyes darting from me
to the door.

"Where is Miss Mattie with the ice?"
she grumbled.

"Here!" cried Mattie,
  bursting into the room.

Father's footsteps thumped
a drumroll on the stairs.

Tears filled my eyes
for fear of his anger and
for the goodness
of being home.

Father was a wide-eyed owl
when he saw me clinging to Ned.
He swooped without a word
across the room,
taking me in his arms
to the kitchen table,
where he laid me down atop it,

Father was a wide-eyed owl.

ordering Miss Emily to hold the lamp
close so he could see.

"What in thunder is going on?"
asked Mother as she leaned close
in the lamplight. "Wherever have you
all been in the middle of the night?"

"It's Emily to blame," Miss Emily said.
"Please, Reverend and Mrs. Jenkins,
do not assume
these innocent children
who merely love to play
are at fault.
It's all My Doing,
this foolish escapade."

15 · Doc Gridley

"Sprained, not broken,
and lucky for you, young Mac,"
said Doc Gridley
as he wrapped my ankle
in a long strip of cloth
the next morning.

"A wise decision
to ice it directly after. . . ."

Doc's hands stopped
along with his words.
He tilted his chin
down toward his chest,
looking over his spectacles
directly at Mother and Father.

Then, flashing a wink and a smile
at me, he finished:
"Directly after the incident —
I mean accident, of course.

"Best you stay
off this foot
a fortnight, Mac.
You'll be running
about town as usual,
you and your friends,
in two weeks' time."

TWO weeks' time!
I said in my head.
The circus is TOMORROW.
I won't see the performance.
I won't see Miz Rozalia
if I have to stay —

"Continue with the ice
for the remainder of the day,
won't you, Mrs. Jenkins?"
Doc Gridley was saying.

"MacGregor!" Father said sternly.
"The doctor is on his way.

Did you lose all knowledge
of proper behavior
in the meadow last night?"

Indeed, Mother and Doc Gridley
were at the door of my room,
stepping into the hallway.

I called out,
"Thank you, Doctor."

"You're most welcome, young man,"
he called back.

16 · The Pastor's Son

I stared at the ceiling,
biting my lip,
trying with all my might
not to cry.

Father cleared his throat —
two quick, gruff huffs —
the same short sound
that announces the start
of his Sunday sermon.

"Close your eyes, Mac,"
he said. "I want you to listen,
and I want you to listen well."

A small breeze
parted the curtains,
tickling my arms
as it passed into the room,
carrying the scent of cut grass.

"You are a fine boy, Mac —
and I want you to know
how much and how often
I admire your courage to do
what you have never done before.
You were brave when you climbed the tree
to bring down Caroline Hill's cat.
You were brave when you
spoke for the Whalen boy
wrongly accused of stealing.

"You are smart,
so I know you
will understand
how important
it is for you —
the pastor's son —
to behave well
in this world,
for on occasions like this —
when you do not behave well —

all the townsfolk will doubt
not just you
but also me."

Why would they do that? I wondered.

Father continued:
"If the people in this town
who trust me
are to listen
when I tell them
what makes a good choice,
they will wonder why
my own boy
makes a carefree choice —
without considering
its consequence.

"Do not mistake me, Mac.
I was a boy. I understand
the lure of adventure.
But, Mac —
you must remember
that even when you are tempted
by someone you like and respect . . ."

Oh, how awful, I thought,
he is blaming Miss Emily.

"Even when someone invites you
to break the rules, MacGregor . . .
Even when that person
is someone you love and trust . . ."

I squeezed my eyes,
and a pattern of wiggly lines
marched across the dark of my eyelids.
I felt a great heavy stone
resting on my chest.

"A pastor's son,
 no matter how young,
 even at ten years old,
 has a responsibility
 to show the people in our church
 how to behave.
 When you forget this, Mac,
 you become injured —
 sometimes in body,
 always in spirit —
 and I become injured, too."

My tears burst out of my eyes
like the Mill River waterfall.
Father leaned over me
and held me while I cried.

I had never considered
that I could hurt Father . . .
or Miss Emily.

I never wanted to do that again.

17 · Visitors

I slept through morning
and awoke to the sight of Mother
standing at the foot of my bed,
a luncheon tray in her hands.

As she placed it on my lap,
she nodded toward a small folded
piece of paper tied with ribbon
to a bouquet of forget-me-nots
next to my plate.

Please, Sir, it read,
do allow this vessel of regret
an afternoon visit if you are well enough.
Your devoted friend —
    no longer queen of any place,
        Miss E.

The sun slanted through my window
late that afternoon. As promised,
there was a slight tapping on my door,
which opened to reveal not only
Miss Emily's wide brown eyes
but behind her,
Ned and Mattie
and Sally.

"Thank you, dear Mac,
  for granting this audience,"
said Miss Emily, bowing low
at the foot of my bed.
She rose slowly. And when
she was again at full height,
she glanced at the ceiling,
shook her head,
and blinked,
as she often did,
seeming to journey fast
back to this world
from far away.

"Here's my hat," said Ned,
  handing me his favorite floppy felt.
"You'll heal faster if you wear it."

Seeming to journey fast back to this world from far away

"It's the end of Edward's story!" said Mattie.
"Aunt Emily is going to tell the rest
  of the story she started at Big Beech."

Miss Emily nodded,
her eyes fixed on the floor
as she sat on the chair
next to my bed.
Her thin hands
slid over the lap of her dress,
smoothing its wrinkles
with two quick strokes.

"Yes," she said,
  glancing at the three of us,
"where were we in the story
  when that whistle blew?"

"John Bill, Edward's trainer,
  had agreed to teach him
  how to fly!" I offered.

"So he did," said Miss Emily,
  a smile flickering across her face.
"Hmm . . . let me see. . . .

"Yes, they did commence
   the work of Edward's dream,
   but it was, from the start,
   impossible for a horse
   to grasp a trapeze.
   Hooves, you know,
   do not have fingers."

In my mind I saw a pair of large
   white gloves on horses' hooves
   and laughed till Miss Emily coughed,
   her eyes resting on me
   above her cupped hand
   hiding her smile.

"John Bill took Edward to a field
   and taught him how to jump over
   taller and taller barricades
   until one day,
   to his great satisfaction,
   Edward cleared a fence
   as high as John Bill.
   A warm wind brushed
   against his belly.
   His hooves felt light.

"'Soaring!' cried Edward.
'I AM SOARING!'

"'And now, indeed,
 you are ready for the boy,' said John Bill,
'for Edward, my friend,
 you shall carry
 a standing boy
 dressed as Mercury
 on your back,
 and the crowd shall behold . . .
 no less than a god's own speed!'"

Miss Emily raised her eyebrows
and rolled her eyes toward
the corner of my room,
her smile a ribbon curling.

"Edward laughed his horse guffaw,"
 she went on. "He was so pleased,
 he snorted till his sides ached.

"Night after night,
 Edward pranced
 around the circus ring
 with the boy Mercury
 balanced on his back.

"Whenever Edward leaped,
  the boy's feet planted
  on his back like moss,
  a great gasp rippled
  through the tent.

"Again and again
  the horse and boy
  pleased the crowd
  until one night
  as they gathered speed
  circling the ring

for the third time,
the boy sneezed
three hollering sneezes,
startling Edward
whose body writhed in midair,
jerking and lurching,
as he tried to get
his floundering feet
upon the ground.

"'The boy! Is the boy safe?'
he whinnied loudly as he landed —
most fortunately on his side.

"'Lady Luck —
as kind to him as you,'
replied John Bill.
'The boy landed on a heap of hay!'

"Thereafter, however,
John Bill would not allow
Edward and the boy to fly.

"'Too risky for two o' me favorites,'
John said. 'Flying Mercury and
ye'll be just as fine trotting
here on the solid earth.'

"Edward sighed.
'I understand.' He nodded,
  looking into John Bill's sad blue eyes.

"'My dream knew some success,' said Edward.
'I have known the birds' delight,
  and that is more than I knew before.'

"Edward's wide black lips pulled back,
  revealing his great gleaming teeth,
  and he laughed his hearty horse guffaw."

Miss Emily stood.
She met my eyes with hers
and bent her knee and head
in a quick curtsy before
swishing out of the room.

Ned and Mattie, Sally and I
looked at one another.
No one spoke for a few moments.
I didn't want Edward to stay on the ground.
I wanted him to fly forever.

"Edward didn't really make
  his dream come true," said Mattie.

"He didn't fly. He jumped!
  Any horse can be trained to jump!"

"He got as close to flying
  as a horse ever could!" said Ned.

"He *was* flying," said Sally.
"And he was kind.
  He cared about the boy's safety
  even when he was in danger himself."

  Mattie frowned
  and pulled a small piece of paper
  from her pocket.

"Aunt Emily told me to read this
  once she'd left."

"DEAR BOYS,
  Please never grow up, which is 'much better —'
  Please never improve — you are perfect now.
      EMILY"

Please never grow up.

18 · Surprise

I heard Mother, Father, and Sally
speaking softly as they ate
at the long dining table.
My own supper was spread
across my lap on a wooden tray.
I wondered how long it would be
before I could join them downstairs.

I looked at my palm.
Some lines were longer and deeper
than others, and I wondered again
how Miz Rozalia could see
my future from looking at those lines.

I remembered Miss Emily
sitting right here
in my room this afternoon.

"She was here," I whispered
to the corner she had gazed into
before she started the story.

"You saw her!" I said,
as if the corner would fold
in on itself and nod in agreement.

Miss Emily hadn't gone
anywhere in years.
She stayed inside the Mansion,
her garden, and her meadows.
She had never crossed
the road to this house
in my memory.

I looked at the two notes
she'd sent to me today.
Her slanted, loopy handwriting
somehow brought her smile
to my mind.

The *clack-clack-clack*
of Father's steps
on the wooden hallway floor
announced his hurried coming
before I saw him at the door.

He looked directly at me and away,
sinking his hands into his pockets,
as he scanned the room.

What is he looking for? I wondered,
waiting for him to speak.

Father pulled out his watch,
read the time,
and cleared his throat
with two short huffs
and a cough.

"The carriage is nearly ready,"
he announced.

Sally's face appeared behind him,
eyes wide, her heels lifting
up and down so she bobbed
like a baby duck behind
its mother in a pond.

Father put his hand atop her shoulder
and sternly fixed his gaze on me.

"I am certain you heard
and understood me
this morning, Mac.
Confinement to the house
for the fortnight ahead
is a fitting consequence.
As is your ankle's pain—
a fine reminder
of a lesson learned.

"However, because . . .
there is a special circumstance
involved in this historic mishap . . .
something . . . that happens rarely
in this town . . ."

"Father's taking us to the circus!"
Sally announced, running to my bedside.
"We're *all* going to the circus!"

Father nodded—
his broad smile
taking over his whole face.

"But how?" I asked.
"How can I go to the circus?"

"I shall carry you to the buggy,"
answered Father. "And once
we are at the fairgrounds,
you, Master Jenkins,
shall ride atop my shoulders
to keep that ankle safe."

19 · The Parade

Our open carriage
joined a long parade
of townsfolk
stretching east
from the common
toward the fairground.
Horses snorted,
hoofing puffs of dust,
as they trotted slowly
beneath the setting sun
to the annual excitement of
"the unusual and extraordinary,"
as Father liked to say.

I looked up
toward the Mansion

as we passed,
hoping Miss Emily
would see me
on my way
to the circus.

She was there, smiling.
She nodded a slow nod,
held up her open palm
and curled it shut.
Was she wearing
her turban?
I wasn't sure —

she disappeared
too fast to know.

The evening breeze
brought the calliope's
magical music
to our carriage
before we saw
the tent top
in the wide meadow
behind Ballard's farm.
I joined its happy rhythm
with my hands clapping Sally's.

And there,
as our carriage passed beneath
a billowing red-and-gold banner
was the tall, grinning ringmaster
calling us into the fairgrounds,
his voice as smooth as
Mother's chocolate-pudding pie.

"Wel-come, All —
Large and Small —
to the show
you shall never forget —
wild and tamed,

familiar and strange,
straight from the jungle
and the western range —
elephant, buffalo,
horses, and monkeys —
you'll see them all.
Wel-come, All,
Large and Small."

20 · The Great Golden Menagerie

Father lifted me to his shoulders
so I sat tall above the crowd,
a sea of bustling hats below me.
I watched for Miz Rozalia
as we passed the smaller tents,
but I did not find her
before we entered
the long, white sailcloth tent
where the animals were on display.

"Animals of the world! Right here!
Before yer very eyes!" cried a boy
clad in ringmaster clothes so fine,
I wished I were a circus boy.

"Taller than two men —
 the largest elephant in the world,"
 its trainer said. Father stepped
 closer than I would have,
 and that big kind-eyed beast
 lifted its trunk to shake my hand!

 Would it grab me? Pull me down?
 Its head was a small house!

 Father steadied my knees.
"Show your manners, Mac!"
 He laughed. So I reached out
 and took hold of the trunk,
 as flexible as a rubber hose.

 A woman dressed in shiny red
 to match the saddle blankets
 of her six white stallions
 looked up at me on Father's shoulders
 and called out, "Look here,
 Ladies and Gentlemen:
 the Tallest Man on Earth
 has come to see me!"

 Three monkeys who looked alike
 sat on the shoulders

So I reached out and took hold of the trunk.

of three boys who looked alike,
all six chewing peanuts,
throwing shells on the ground.

A crowd so tightly packed
around one stall
made it hard to see
the animal it held.

"A two-horned rhinoceros!"
I called down to Father,
Mother, and Sally.

21 · The Lion King

The bell rang,
inviting us into the pavilion
for the circus show.

I spied Ned and Mattie
seated near us.
They spied us and waved.
Mattie jumped to her feet,
and Mrs. Dickinson spoke,
but I could not hear her words.

The ringmaster introduced the horses
and the beautiful lady in red,
whose whip cracked
and snapped commands
so those horses pranced and bowed

and stood with front legs
on one another's backs in a long row
before they cantered out of the ring.

A lanky man in blue-striped pants
strode before us, pulling a wagon
that held a bright green wooden chest.
From his pocket he took a key,
unlocked the box,
and withdrew a serpent
thick as his arm. It was so long
I wondered when it would end
as it slowly curled around his body
and back inside the box.

"Ladies, Gentlemen! Girls and Boys!"
crowed the ringmaster.
"It is my great pleasure
to introduce you to . . .
the bravest man alive —
the Lion King!"

A muscular man with curly black hair,
dressed as a gladiator
strode into the performance ring.
His sandals were strapped from
his ankles to his knees.

It slowly curled around his body.

His shining gold breastplate
glinted and winked.

In one hand he held a wooden club
while with his other hand
he led a full-grown lion
tethered by a silver chain.

Sally clutched Mother's hand
and sidled close to her with haste.
I was not afraid.
I was certain
the Lion King was captain
of that great tawny beast.

The lion roared
and cocked its head
before it dropped to the ground,
paws extended in front
like an obedient dog.

And there it stayed
still as stone
as the Lion King
pulled forth a fluffy lamb
from the sack he'd carried on his back.

He held the little thing
above his head.

"Will he feed it to the lion?"
Sally asked Mother,
who, like the rest of the crowd,
was stunned with fear
for the helpless creature.

The Lion King turned.
He knelt and gently placed the lamb
between the lion's massive paws.
The lion licked its lips
and licked the lamb
like a mother cat and her kitten!
I cheered a wild whoop of relief
with the rest of the crowd,
standing on our feet.

A young boy took the lamb.
The Lion King strode in circles
round the beast, at last squatting
straight before it, staring eye to eye.

He placed his own wide hands
upon each side of the lion's head,

talking to it all this time,
his voice so soft
we could not hear his words.

The Lion King
slowly
pulled
the lion's
mouth
open.

"Goodness!" whispered Mother,
"Who wants to see those teeth?"

Me, I thought.

Those gleaming sharp teeth
were as long
as the Lion King's fingers!
He pulled the jaws apart
so wide, I thought of a cave.
The King leaned
toward the beast,
close and closer,
till his head
was half inside that wild place
for a moment so long,

the whole tent gaped,
caught by fear
until the Lion King let go,
jumped backward,
and flipped over to an upright stand,
his arms overhead in a triumphant V,
and the great menacing
lion mouth was closed.

I don't know what came next
or after that, as all I could see
in my mind during
the rest of the show
was the Lion King.

Under the bright stars
on the way home,
the carriage slowly jiggling
my red-hot, aching ankle,
I thought of Miss Emily's face
when I would tell her
of tonight's excitement —
the elephant and the horses,
the snake and the Lion King.
I knew her eyes would widen
and roll to the side. She would
giggle and proclaim surprise,
and I thought of something
I'd never thought before.

She needs our eyes
to see these things for her,
for — playful as she is with us —
she isn't part of the world's hubbub
anymore. She is getting old!

22 · Watching the Rain

It rained every day for a week.

"Pouring from a heavenly pitcher,"
Mother said.

"Northampton Bridge is closed,
the river's so high," Father reported.

Sally and I played games
and watched horses slide
in the mud, pulling carriages
toward town. We watched
umbrellas bob toward the train station,
and I wondered where Miz Rozalia
and the Lion King might be by now.

Again and again,
Sally asked when we were alone,
"Tell the story of the Circus Night."

Every morning I hummed the
calliope's tune as I turned my ankle
side to side and up and down
just the way Doc Gridley had advised.
Each day I moved it a bit more with less pain.
By week's end, I was able to walk slowly.

"Well enough to come down to dinner,"
said Mother, smiling.

"Well enough to resume some chores,"
said Father.

Still, I was housebound
like a winter bee in the hive
till Doc Gridley's proclamation
of two weeks' confinement
had been met.

It rained every day for a week.

23 · The Upstairs Circus

I knocked on Ned's door.

"Mac, my friend,
please hasten inside!
You are invited to join us
upstairs at the Evergreens
for a premiere performance!"

Ned swept his arm
toward the front hall,
where the light,
always dim,
demanded a moment
for my eyes to adjust.

I took the stairs slowly
while Ned strode

two at a time to the top,
turning sharply
as he placed a tattered
tall hat atop his head.

"Wel-come, All, Large and Small,
to the show you shall never forget!"
he called, opening the door
to the back wing of the house.

"It's the circus train,
don't you see?" said Ned,
tilting his head toward
the long narrow hallway.

"Here are the cars.
One for the animals,
one for performers,
and one for the trainers
and animal feeders."

Ned was right.
The children's hallway,
where we'd played so many times,
very clearly resembled a train.
His and Mattie's small rooms
and the nursery, all opening

Ned was right.

to this narrow passage,
were perfectly located
and properly sized
to be railcars.

"Wel-come, All,
Large and Small!"
boomed Ned.
"Ladies and Gentlemen!
Girls and Boys of all ages!
May I present . . .
Miss Swiftly, the Exotic
half-girl, half-bird from the
blistering-hot, dripping
Amazon Jungle!"

Mattie ran into the hall
on her toes, arms uplifted,
feathers fluttering.
She waved and bowed,
twirling and squawking
as if she'd been on the stage
her whole life.

"And . . . for your pleasure . . .
the one and only
bareback equestrian

capable of handstands
atop her horse —
none other than our own
Sal the Gal and her team
of wild stallions!
Sally cantered into the hall
from Mattie's room,
with a hop-step-hop,
pulling Carlo behind her
attached to a braided ribbon,
which wrapped round her waist
as she led him in a circle
till the ribbon made her
into a Maypole.

I applauded.
We all laughed.

"Will you join the Upstairs Circus, Mac?"
asked Sally. "Will you be King Boaz?"

I thought for a moment.

"I will join, of course,
but I shall need Carlo.
May I? And . . .
shouldn't we perform

Till the ribbon made her into a Maypole.

next door in the garden
and invite Miss Emily?"

"Indeed, sir, you are correct."
Ned nodded.

"Why, of course," said Miss Swiftly.

"Yes! Yes! The best of plans!"
squealed Sal the Gal.

24 · The Greatest Show of All

A gray-white sky,
the prickly air, and
the leaves rising in the trees
told us a storm was near,
urging us to hurry.

"I shall invite her!"
announced Mattie,
running ahead on the path.

"I feel rain," said Sally.

"Bring her to the barn, Miss Swiftly,"
called Ned. "Ask Aunt Vinnie
to come, too. We'll arrange
a place for them to sit."

Ned and I dragged a bale of hay
onto the wide plank floor
between the two lower lofts.

"We'll perform here," said Ned,
  pointing to the back wall.
"All barn cats and kittens,
  the mice and their mothers
  and brothers and sisters,
  can peek from the high loft
  while here, the guests of honor
  will sit directly before us."

"Get your horse ready, Sal," I said.
"As soon as you're finished with your act,
  pass Carlo to me offstage."

Mattie skipped into the barn,
  her cheeks red and glistening
  from the rain.

"They are coming! Quickly!
  Aunt Emily *and* Aunt Vinnie!"

I whispered my plan to Ned
  as he covered the bale

with a blanket, and I rolled
my pants up to my knees.

First, Mattie —
I mean Miss Swiftly —
and Sal the Gal performed,
Carlo the perfect black stallion.
The aunts stood as they clapped,
Miss Emily cheering, "Bravo!"
Miss Vinnie stomped her feet,
whistling shrill through her teeth.

Ned strode back to center stage,
bowed, and proclaimed,
"Ladies! Please!
Take hold of your hats.
I now have the great pleasure
to present for the first time
in the history of the world . . .
a performer who will
without question
make the hair on your head
stand up, stiffen, and shake!"

Miss Emily's eyes crinkled.
She quickly placed her hands
upon her head,

nodding to Miss Vinnie
to secure her own imaginary hat.

Mattie and Sally giggled as they ran
to Miss Emily and Miss Vinnie
and sat at their feet.

Ned continued.
"You are about to witness
the Bravest Man on Earth,
known far and wide
as King of Kings,
Master of the Ferocious,
here today with lion in tow —
King Boaz!"

I stroked Carlo's ears
and led him onto the stage.

"Your club!" cried Ned,
handing me an umbrella.

I took the umbrella
and laid it upon the floor.
"No need for this!" I announced.
"My beast knows who is in charge!"
I kneeled beside Carlo.

Miss Emily's tinkling laugh
made Carlo's ears twitch.
He smiled at her
as I placed my hands
on his wet snout and jaw
and pulled them slowly apart.

"Oh, no!" cried Mattie.
"Don't put your head
  in that slobbery cave!"

"I must," I whispered to Carlo.
"And you, sir, must do as I say,
  for we are, my friend,
  about to fly like Edward,
  looking for our dream."

The crowd hushed.
  I tilted my head toward Carlo's mouth,
  whispering again and again,
"Good dog, good boy," the whole time,
  and when I pulled my face away
  and stood, the crowd cheered us
  with "How brave!"
  and "How awful!"
  and "How did he do it?"

25 · The Last Act

"Performers return to the stage,"
called Ned. "If you please!
Curtain call! Curtain call!"

In the excitement
of Miss Swiftly and Sal
climbing back onto the stage,
the five of us aligning ourselves
in one straight row,
no one, as usual, saw
Miss Emily's dash
from her first-row seat
to the loft, where
still unseen to us,
she called out,
"Ringmaster! Please!
There is one final act

The five of us aligning ourselves in one straight row

that must be performed
before the show is done!"

"Yes, why, yes, of course,"
cried Ned.
"The Greatest Show of All
is proud, most proud,
to present the rarely seen
day or night,
here or there,
now or then . . .
Queen Prosperina,
here this day
in the Dickinson barn theatre
on the second level —
our finale! This show's
own Queen Prosperina!"

I looked up, and there
on the edge of the high loft
above us was Miss Emily,
her hair wrapped inside her shawl.

Miss Vinnie drew in her breath
so strong she sounded
like a broom sweeping
sand across the floor.

Queen Prosperina,
standing tall
nodded to me,
catching my eyes with hers
wide and sure.

"This performance
is dedicated to you,
my courageous king,
you, sir,
Boaz the Brave!"

She paused. She bowed.
She stepped out of view,
then reappeared, running
toward the edge of the loft,
holding the thick barn rope
in her grasp as she swung
her stockinged legs up
and around the rope,
out into the air above us,
straddling the knot
at the base of the rope
until she was over
the opposite loft,
where she let go
and leaped into the air,

laughing as she landed.
Then standing,
smoothing her skirt
and her hair now wildly
framing her face
as she said, most solemnly,

"We never know how high we are
 Till we are called to rise
 And then if we are true to plan
 Our statures touch the skies."

Miss Emily swung her arm toward us,
giggling, full of breath, and bowed.

"Bravo!" I called, "to our own
 daring and dear Circus Queen!"

Historical Notes

Emily Dickinson (December 10, 1830–May 15, 1886) is considered the most famous woman poet in America. She wrote nearly 1,800 poems, of which only ten were published during her lifetime. Of the notes attributed to her pen in this novel, only the one beginning "Dear Boys" on page 82 was actually written by her. The lines Miss Emily recites after she soars across the barn ("We never know how high we are . . .") are from poem number J 1176/F 1197 in *The Poems of Emily Dickinson*.

MacGregor (Mac) Jenkins (1867–1940) wrote several books, journal articles, and stories as an adult. He lived across the street from the Dickinson mansion during part of his childhood. His book *Emily Dickinson, Friend and Neighbor* was published in 1930.

EDWARD (NED) DICKINSON (1862–1898), Emily Dickinson's nephew, was born and lived in Amherst, Massachusetts, next door to his aunt.

MARTHA (MATTIE) DICKINSON BIANCHI (1866–1943) grew up to write several books about her famous aunt, including a collection of her aunt's letters as well as recollections of her own childhood.

REVEREND JONATHAN L. JENKINS (1830–1913), Mac and Sally's father, was pastor of the First Congregational Church in Amherst, Massachusetts, from 1867 to 1877. He was a close friend of the Dickinson family.

ISAAC VAN AMBURGH, THE LION KING (1808–1865), was born in Kentucky, where at a very young age he became known as a gifted communicator with animals. By the time he was in his twenties, he was known on both sides of the Atlantic as the boldest of lion trainers who placed his own head between a lion's jaws. At one point, he trained a young girl to stand on the back of a lion while holding a lamb in her arms as he placed another lamb between the lion's paws. Van Amburgh eventually purchased his own menagerie, which carried his name long after his death.

Van Amburgh & Company's Great Golden Menagerie and Frost's Roman Circus and Royal Coliseum came to Amherst in June 1877. Advertisements for the circus proclaimed 175 horses, 56 wagons, five of the world's champion riders, bareback somersaulting equestrians, a contortionist "rubber man," the largest elephant in the world, and a two-horned rhinoceros. Admission to both circus and menagerie was fifty cents.

John Bill Ricketts, famed for his skill as a performing equestrian in Britain, brought his circus to the United States in 1793. President George Washington is said to have been so impressed when Ricketts's horse leaped over ten horses with a boy on its shoulders that he sold Ricketts his aging horse Jack for display in Ricketts's circus, which toured to New York and Boston. Ricketts's circus had a permanent home in Philadelphia, where it was housed in a large white coliseum topped by a weathervane in the shape of Mercury, messenger of the gods.

Flying Mercury. John Bill Ricketts took to the ring of his own circus as he rode horseback dressed as Mercury with his young son balanced on his shoulders. Andrew Ducrow was another famous British circus equestrian who was often costumed as Mercury while circling the performance ring on horseback.

BIBLIOGRAPHY

Amherst (MA) Record. June 29, 1877.

Benfey, Christopher, Polly Longsworth, and Barton Levi St. Armand. *The Dickinsons of Amherst.* Hanover, NH: University Press of New England, 2001.

Bianchi, Martha Dickinson. *Emily Dickinson, Face to Face.* Cambridge, MA: Riverside Press/Houghton Mifflin, 1932.

———. *The Life and Letters of Emily Dickinson.* Boston: Houghton Mifflin, 1924.

Chindahl, George L. *A History of the Circus in America.* Caldwell, ID: Caxton Printers, 1959.

Croft-Cooke, Rupert, and Peter Cotes. *Circus: A World History*. London: Elek, 1976.

Culhane, John. *The American Circus: An Illustrated History*. New York: Henry Holt, 1990.

Dickinson, Emily. *The Poems of Emily Dickinson*. Edited by R. W. Franklin. Cambridge, MA: Belknap Press/Harvard University Press, 1998.

Gruen, Sara. *Water for Elephants*. Chapel Hill, NC: Algonquin, 2006.

Habegger, Alfred. *My Wars Are Laid Away in Books: The Life of Emily Dickinson*. New York: Random House, 2001.

Jenkins, MacGregor. *Emily Dickinson, Friend and Neighbor*. Boston: Little, Brown, 1930.

Leyda, Jay. *The Years and Hours of Emily Dickinson*. New Haven, CT: Yale University Press, 1960.

Lombardo, Daniel. *A Hedge Away: The Other Side of Emily Dickinson's Amherst*. Northampton, MA: Daily Hampshire Gazette, 1977.

Longsworth, Polly. *The World of Emily Dickinson*. New York: Norton, 1990.

Loxton, Howard. *The Golden Age of the Circus*. New York: Smithmark, 1997.

MacMurray, Rose. *Afternoons with Emily*. New York: Little, Brown, 2007.

Sewall, Richard B. *The Life of Emily Dickinson*. Cambridge, MA: Harvard University Press, 1994.

Verney, Peter. *Here Comes the Circus*. New York: Paddington Press, 1978.

Ward, Theodora Van Wagenen. *Emily Dickinson's Letters to Dr. and Mrs. Josiah Gilbert Holland*. Cambridge, MA: Harvard University Press, 1951.

ACKNOWLEDGMENTS

This joyful work would not have happened without the enthusiastic encouragement of its first astute readers — my son, Bjorn Mutén, and my grandson, Jonas Eichenlaub, whose careful listening led us to many excited conversations about the content of this book.

I am grateful to Polly Longsworth, Jeanne Shumway, Fanny Rothschild, Jeannine Atkins, Peggy Ann White, Michele De Cresce, Joan Bredin-Price, Theresa Atteridge, and Catherine Iselin for their thoughtful comments and belief in this book. To my inspiring and patient writing-group members, Ann Desmond, Michelle Kwasney, Marvin Ellin, and Nancy Carpenter, I place my hands together and bow. For Rozalia and years of inspiration, my heartfelt thanks to Giselle Sharaf.

Many thanks to Jane Wald, Cindy Dickinson, and Nan Fishlein of the Emily Dickinson Museum for inviting me to participate in the annual summer children's circus events at the museum, where I was able to hear the laughter of children in the place where Mac, Mattie, Ned, and Sally actually played. Special thanks to my former kindergarten student Lily Wear for suggesting that Emily Dickinson's love of the smallest creatures was so keen, she might even have written a poem in honor of slugs.